THUD!

For Annette.
My best friend.

THUD!

NICK BUTTERWORTH

PictureLions
An Imprint of HarperCollins*Publishers*

Basil the bushbaby yawned. He had not had a good night's sleep. The arrival in the middle of the night of the mysterious Ugly Beast had disturbed just about everyone.

Now Basil fancied a snooze in the sunshine. He tied a small hammock between two stumpy trees and climbed in. Soon he began to doze.
But not for long. . .

THUD!

Basil opened one eye. Something was making the ground shake.

THUD!

There it was again. Stronger this time.
Basil's hammock began to sway.

THUD. . .THUD!

"W-w-what's happening?" said Basil, as his hammock bounced up and down.

THUD. . .THUD. . .THUD!

The ground shook terribly and Basil was bounced right out of his hammock. Suddenly, a great shadow passed over him.

THUD...THUD...THUD...THUD!

"Oh no! Oh dear!" he squeaked in fright.
"It's a m—m—monster!"

Basil was right. With great thundering
footsteps, a huge monster went crashing by.
Basil quaked and hid his face.

THUD...THUD...THUD...THUD...THUD!

The footsteps grew fainter. When Basil could hear them no longer, he dared to look. "This is terrible!" he wailed. "First the Ugly Beast and now a monster! I must get help. We must get rid of it."

Spike the porcupine was eating some stickleberries when the bushbaby found him.

"Help! Please help!" cried Basil.

The porcupine quickly pushed the rest of the stickleberries into his mouth.

"How can I help?" he said.

Basil told Spike all about the monster.

"Please," said Basil, "can you make it go away? Your spines look sharp and fierce. I'm sure it would do what you say."

Spike frowned. "No," he said. "I'm not very good at getting rid of monsters. I can do dogs," he said, "and pigs."

Spike thought for a moment. "That gives me an idea," he said. "Follow me."

P iers the warthog was admiring his face
in the pond.

"Excuse us," said the porcupine politely.
"We're having trouble with a monster.
Can you help? We think that if you made a
terrible face and showed your tusks and lots
of sharp teeth. . .we think you could scare
it away."

Piers looked into the pond again. "No, no," he grunted. "That's no job for me. I'm much too beautiful for that, don't you think?" Basil and Spike had to agree.

"But," said the warthog, "I have an idea. Follow me."

The rainbow birds were screeching and squawking at each other in the tangled branches of a tree.

"What a dreadful din," said the warthog. "Quiet, please!" The birds were quiet at once.

"We're having trouble with a monster," said Piers, "and your peckerty beaks are just what we need to drive it away."

THUD...**THUD**...**THUD**...**THUD**...THUD...

The rainbow birds looked worried.
They began to mumble and squawk
together.

"We don't do monsters," said one of the
birds at last. "Try the lion."

"Try the hippopotamus," said another bird.

"Try the crocodile," squawked another.

Ralph the lion couldn't help.
    "I've got a sore throat," he said.
    Delilah, the huge muddy-brown
hippopotamus, was busy.
    "I'm having a bath," she said. "So sorry."

Humphrey the crocodile just moaned.
"Can't help," he said. "Got toothache."
Nobody wanted to face the monster.

They asked the aardvark and the antelope. They asked the zebra and the zorilla. "What shall we do?" said Spike. "We've tried everyone."

"Not quite," said the warthog.
"There is one more that we might ask.
The strange creature who came to the forest
last night."

The creature they called the Ugly Beast was not like anything they had ever seen before. Where it had come from, no one knew. Whether it would be fierce or friendly, they could only guess.

Piers the warthog set off and led the long procession towards the dark forest. There, they came upon the Ugly Beast.

"Please forgive this intrusion," the warthog began, "but we want to get rid of a monster."

"Yes we do, yes we do!" squawked the rainbow birds.

"Look here, old chap, do you think you might frighten it away?" said the lion.

The strange creature looked sad.
"I might," he said, "one day, when I'm
fully grown. But I'm too little now."
Everyone looked disappointed.

THUD. . .THUD. . .THUD. . .THUD. . .THUD. . .

"Wait!" said Basil. "It's simple. None of us can make the monster go away on our own. So, we must all do it together!"

"This is a clever and brilliant idea!" said Ralph the lion. His throat was suddenly much better.

"These great footprints will lead us to the monster," he said. "Come along now. Smallest at the front, tallest at the back. . . just so the monster can see everyone."

THUD. . .**THUD. . .THUD. . .THUD. . .**

The footprints led them past great trees and over the muddy bed of a river.

"That's it! Keep going," called Ralph from the back.

"Look!" squeaked Basil suddenly. "The monster is on the other side of that hill!"

Everyone tip-toed to the top of the hill. There it was, sitting with its back towards them. The monster.

"Go on," said the lion huskily to Basil. His throat had suddenly become sore again.

Basil looked back at everyone. Then, in a very small voice, he spoke to the monster.

"Excuse me. . ."

Only the monster's ears twitched.

"Excuse me," said Basil again, "but we have come to ask you to. . ."

The monster turned.

"I'm sorry. I do beg your pardon," said the monster in a voice that was not at all monstrous. "Were you speaking to me?"

S uddenly, a voice called out from the crowd.

Everybody stared in amazement at the Ugly Beast.

Then the monster beamed a great big smile and shouted out loudly. . .

Everyone was astonished.

Raymond ran to his mother and she hugged him.

"I've been searching everywhere for you," she said.

Then she turned to Basil. "I'm sorry, you were saying something?"

"Umm, well," said Basil, "we came to ask you. . . that is, we wanted to ask you. . ." Basil paused and took a deep breath.

"Will you stay with us?"

Everyone suddenly cheered.

"Can we? Oh please can we stay?" Raymond asked.

"Well," said his mother, "we might. We'll just have to wait 'til your father gets here."

Basil looked at Raymond. Then he looked at Raymond's enormous mother.

"Father. . ." said Basil slowly. "He's got a father. . .

Just wait 'til his father gets here. . ."

THUD!
THUD!
THUD!

First published in hardback in Great Britain by HarperCollins Publishers Ltd. in 1997
First published in Picture Lions in 1998

5 7 9 10 8 6 4
ISBN : 0 00 664646-8

Picture Lions is an imprint of the Children's Division, part of HarperCollins Publishers Ltd.
Text and illustrations copyright © Nick Butterworth 1997
Printed and bound in Singapore by Imago

Nick Butterworth is a designer, artist and author with more than fifty books to his credit. He lives in Suffolk with his wife Annette and their two children, Ben and Amanda.

By Nick Butterworth, published by Collins Children's Books

All Together Now!
When We Play Together • When It's Time for Bed
When There's Work to Do • When We Go Shopping
Amanda's Butterfly

Percy the Park Keeper stories are available in hardback, paperback and audio cassette:

One Snowy Night • After the Storm
The Rescue Party • The Secret Path • The Treasure Hunt

The Fox's Hiccups • The Cross Rabbit • The Badger's Bath
The Hedgehog's Balloon • One Warm Fox • The Owl's Lesson

A Year in Percy's Park • Tales from Percy's Park